Poké

I want to be the very be[st]
To beat all the rest, yea[h]

Catch 'em, Catch 'em, Gotta catch 'em all

Pokémon I'll search across the land
Look far and wide
Release from my hand
The power that's inside

Catch 'em, Catch 'em, Gotta catch 'em all
Pokémon!

Gotta catch 'em all, Gotta catch 'em all
Gotta catch 'em all, Gotta catch 'em all

At least one hundred and fifty or more to see
To be a Pokémon Master is my destiny

Catch 'em, Catch 'em, Gotta catch 'em all
Gotta catch 'em all, Pokémon! (repeat three times)

Can YOU Rap all 150?

**Here's the rest of the Poké Rap.
Catch book #15
Psyduck Ducks Out
for the first 32 Pokémon!**

Dratini, Growlithe, Mr. Mime, Cubone
Graveler, Voltorb, Gloom

Charmeleon, Wartortle
Mewtwo, Tentacruel, Aerodactyl
Omanyte, Slowpoke
Pidgeot, Arbok
That's all folks!

Words and Music by Tamara Loeffler and John Siegler
Copyright © 1999 Pikachu Music (BMI)
Worldwide rights for Pikachu Music administered by Cherry River Music Co. (BMI)
All Rights Reserved   Used by Permission

There are more books
about Pokémon.

Collect them all!

POKéMON™

Talent Showdown

By Tracey West

SCHOLASTIC INC.
New York   Toronto   London   Auckland   Sydney
Mexico City   New Delhi   Hong Kong

For all the Pokémoniacs who keep me inspired:
Pokémon Master Terry, Lauren, Alex, Michael, Sam,
and everyone who sends me letters and pictures.
Thanks! — T.W.

No part of this publication may be reproduced in whole or in part, or stored in a retrieval system, or transmitted in any form or by any means, electronic, mechanical, photocopying, recording, or otherwise, without written permission of the publisher. For information regarding permission, write to Scholastic Inc., Attention: Permissions Department, 555 Broadway, New York, NY 10012.

ISBN 0-439-20090-3

12 11 10 9 8 7 6 5 4 3 2 1   0 1 2 3 4 5/0

Printed in the U.S.A.

First Scholastic printing, November 2000

The World of Pokémon

Indigo
Plateau

Pewter
City

Mt. Moon

Celadon
City

Cerulean
City

Sea
Cottage

Saffron
City

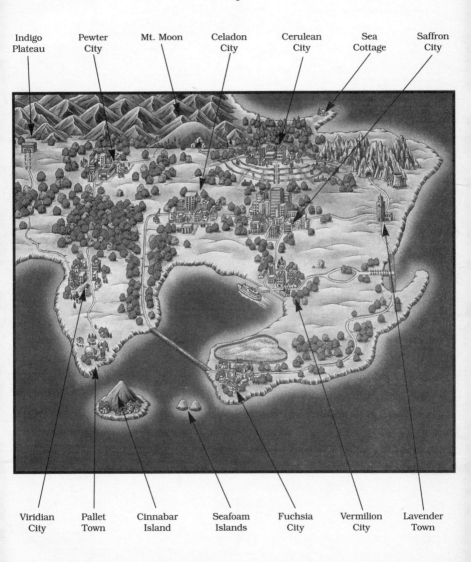

Viridian
City

Pallet
Town

Cinnabar
Island

Seafoam
Islands

Fuchsia
City

Vermilion
City

Lavender
Town

Gary, again!

"This town sure is crowded," Ash Ketchum said. "I wonder what's going on?"

Ash and his friends Misty and Brock had wandered into the town to find food and a place to sleep. Together they were on a journey to capture and train Pokémon, creatures with amazing powers.

Orange-haired Misty hugged Togepi, a baby Pokémon, close to her. "This place is a little too noisy for me," Misty said. "Togepi could use a nap."

"*Togi! Togi!*" cooed the Pokémon. Togepi

flapped its tiny arms. They stuck out of the colorful eggshell that covered its body.

"*Pikachu!*" agreed Pikachu, Ash's Pokémon. The yellow lightning mouse always walked alongside its trainer.

Brock scanned the crowded street. "I don't know if we'll find a quiet place in this town," said the older boy. "But maybe we can find out what's going on."

"Good idea," Ash said. A boy his age stood nearby. The boy had six red-and-white Poké Balls attached to a belt around his waist. Ash recognized him as a fellow Pokémon trainer. He approached the boy.

"What's happening in this town?" Ash asked. "Some kind of Pokémon competition?" Ash hoped that was true. He never missed a chance to battle other Pokémon trainers. It was the best way to get experience.

"Something like that," the boy replied. He pointed to a large building down the street. "That's where all the action is."

"Great!" Ash said. He turned to his friends. "Let's check it out!"

Misty sighed. "Okay, Ash. But we've got to rest soon. Togepi is getting cranky."

Ash didn't reply. He was too busy charging down the street. Pikachu ran at his heels.

Ash skidded to a stop in front of the large, white building. It looked like some kind of theater. A wooden sign above the door read REHEARSAL HALL.

"This is an unusual place for a Pokémon battle," Ash told Pikachu.

"Pika!" Pikachu nodded.

Ash opened the doors, and he and Pikachu stepped inside. The room was crowded with trainers and Pokémon.

But the Pokémon weren't battling.

In fact, Ash thought they were acting kind of strange.

A girl in a white tuxedo jacket and skirt was throwing colorful balls to Seel, a Water Pokémon. The Seel caught the balls on its nose, one by one.

A boy in a sparkling suit was tap dancing and singing a song. Farfetch'd, a Flying Pokémon, danced along to the music.

A girl in a karate uniform was doing a karate routine with Machop, a fighting Pokémon.

All over the room, Pokémon and their trainers were singing, dancing, and doing tricks.

Misty and Brock caught up to Ash.

"What's going on here?" Ash asked his friends. "I've never seen anything like it."

Before they could answer, a nasal voice interrupted.

"So, Ash, we meet again." A boy with spiky brown hair stood there. The boy wore a long-sleeved blue shirt and jeans. Behind him, a group of girls wearing cheerleader uniforms and carrying pom-poms waved and smiled at Ash.

"Gary!" Ash said in disbelief. He and Gary grew up together in Pallet Town. They had started their Pokémon journeys at the same time. Gary was Ash's greatest rival. He and Ash were always trying to outdo each other.

"So you're entering the Pokémon Talent Show, are you?" Gary asked. "There must be a mistake. This isn't a Talent*less* Show. That's the show you should be entering."

Ash frowned. "Gary, why are you still giving me a hard time? I thought that was over when I did better than you in the Pokémon League Tournament."

Every trainer's dream was to become a member of the Pokémon League. To get in, you had to battle lots of other trainers. Ash and Gary had both competed at the same tournament.

Gary laughed. "Is that what you think? The way I see it, you're still a loser. After all, you didn't win."

Ash felt his face flush with anger. Brock put a hand on his shoulder.

Misty jumped into the conversation. "So,

Gary, tell us about the talent show."

"Haven't you heard?" Gary replied. "The competition is for trainers and their Pokémon. You're judged on how entertaining the act is, how well your Pokémon are trained, and how well you perform as a trainer. All of the best trainers compete."

"So what's your act?" Misty asked.

Gary beamed proudly. "It's only the most spectacular stage show ever. I'll be singing a song I wrote called 'Gary Is the Greatest.' It'll have fireworks, cheer-

leaders, and a dancing chorus line of all my Pokémon."

"Gary is the greatest!" the cheerleaders cheered.

"So what's your act, Ash?" Gary sneered. "Or are you just going to stand onstage and beg the judges for pity?"

Ash felt his blood boil. Gary was too much. He had to show Gary that he was no loser, once and for all.

"I have a fantastic act planned," Ash said. "Much better than your stupid song. It's going to blow the judges away!"

"I'll believe it when I see it, Ash," Gary said. He and the cheerleaders walked away, laughing.

"You really stood up for yourself," Brock said. "Good for you."

"Yeah!" Ash said.

Misty shook her head. "Uh, Ash, there's only one problem," she said.

"What's that?" Ash asked.

"You don't have an act!" Misty said.

Persian VS. Squirtle

"I've got plenty of talent," Ash said. "I'm a great Pokémon trainer. I caught a Snorlax, didn't I? And a Lapras. I bet nobody here can say that."

"Maybe not," Misty said. "But they can sing and dance and do tricks. That's what *this* competition is about."

Ash frowned. "I guess you're right," he said. He looked around the rehearsal hall at the Pokémon and their trainers.

One boy was throwing balls to an Exeggutor, a three-headed Pokémon. The

Exeggutor was catching the balls with its feet.

A girl was doing a comedy act in one corner of the room. Next to her, a Haunter laughed at all her jokes.

Ash turned to Pikachu. "We can do this together, Pikachu," Ash said. "There must be something you can do. Can you sing?"

Pikachu shook its head.

"Can you dance?" Ash asked.

Pikachu shook its head.

Ash tried again. "Can you juggle?"

Pikachu shook its head a third time.

"You must have some special talent," Ash said.

"Pika!" Pikachu smiled. Tiny sparks flew from its bright red cheeks. The yellow Pokémon aimed a small electric charge at Ash.

"Aaaaaaaaah!" Ash cried as the electricity tingled through his body. "Pikachu, that's not what I had in mind!"

"Pikachu," Pikachu apologized.

Misty and Brock couldn't help laughing.

"That's what I call a *shocking* act!" Misty said between giggles.

9

Dejected, Ash walked away from his friends. "I'll think of something," Ash called back over his shoulder. "You'll see."

Ash sank down on the edge of a small portable swimming pool. He held his face in his hands.

I've got to find a way to win this competition, Ash thought to himself. *I've got to beat Gary somehow.*

"What have you done with my Seel?"

Ash snapped to attention at the sound of the angry voice. It belonged to a girl about his age. She had curly brown hair, and wore a costume — a white tuxedo jacket and a skirt. On the back of her jacket the words SALLY AND HER AMAZING SEEL were written in sequins.

"Where is it?" Sally asked him.

"I don't know what you're talking about," Ash said. "I didn't touch your Seel."

"It was here in this pool a few minutes ago," Sally said. "We were practicing our act. I went to get a drink of water, and now it's gone."

"That's too bad," Ash said. "But I —"

"Save your story," Sally said angrily. "There's only one way to solve this."

Sally took a red-and-white Poké Ball from her jacket pocket.

"I challenge you to a battle against my performing Pokémon," she said. "Two Pokémon each." She threw the ball into the air. "Persian, you're on!" Sally cried.

A sleek, white Pokémon that looked like

a jungle cat burst forth in a blaze of light. Persian had a round red jewel in the middle of its forehead. Ash had never battled a Persian before. He thought quickly.

"Squirtle, I choose you!" Ash threw a Poké Ball and a Pokémon that looked like a turtle appeared. Squirtle was cute, but Ash knew it had powerful Water Attacks.

Sally didn't hesitate to launch Persian's attack.

"Persian, Growl!" Sally ordered the Pokémon.

A snarl crossed Persian's face. A low, rumbling growl started in its throat. Persian opened its mouth and the growl poured out.

Squirtle covered its ears with its hands. It started to lose its balance.

"What's happening?" Ash asked.

Sally smiled. "Growl lowers an opponent's attack power," she said. "Now

Persian's ready for its next attack. Persian, Bite!"

Squirtle fell to the ground weakened.

Persian bared its sharp teeth. Then it sprung into the air.

"No!" Ash cried.

3

Seel's Disappearing Act

"Squirtle! Water Gun fast!" Ash cried.

Squirtle struggled to stand up. Persian lunged toward the Water Pokémon, ready to sink its teeth into Squirtle's arm.

Just in time, Squirtle shot a forceful blast of water right at Persian. The water pushed Persian back. The classy cat Pokémon thudded to the floor. Its prized fur dripped water.

Persian hissed at Squirtle.

"I never met a cat that liked taking a bath!" Ash said.

Misty, Brock, and Pikachu ran up.

"What's going on?" Brock asked.

"You guys are just in time," Ash said. He held out Squirtle's Poké Ball.

"Squirtle, return!" Ash called out.

Squirtle disappeared into the ball.

Ash turned to Pikachu. "Finish this up, Pikachu. Squirtle's water will help conduct your electricity!"

"Pika pika!" Pikachu said, nodding. It closed its eyes, building up an electric charge in its body.

"Pikachuuuuuuu!"

Pikachu hurled a thunderbolt at the

soggy Persian. The catlike Pokémon lit up with the charge. Then it sank to the floor in a heap.

Sally ran to her Pokémon's side.

"Persian, are you okay?" she asked.

"We can end this battle now if you want," Ash said. "I'm telling you, I didn't take your Seel."

"Is that what this is about?" Misty asked. She turned to Sally. "Ash would never steal someone's Pokémon."

Sally sighed. She stroked the Persian, which purred quietly. Then she took out Persian's Poké Ball.

"Show's over, Persian," she said, and Persian returned to its ball.

Sally faced Ash.

"I'm sorry, Ash. I just got too upset when I saw that Seel was missing," Sally said. "Seel was the first Pokémon I ever caught. It's more than a Pokémon to me. It's a good friend."

Ash knew what Sally meant. He couldn't imagine how he would feel if anything ever happened to Pikachu.

"I understand," Ash said. "Why don't you tell me exactly what happened? Maybe we can figure out where Seel is."

Sally smiled weakly. "Thanks," she said. "I told you, I left the pool to get a drink of water. When I came back, Seel was gone."

"Did you see anything unusual?" Brock asked her.

Sally seemed thoughtful. Then her eyes lit up. "I didn't see anything," she said. "But I did hear something. There was some really strange music playing."

Ash looked at the performers who filled the room. "There are a lot of strange sounds in this place right now."

Sally shook her head. "It wasn't like normal music. It was kind of . . . creepy."

Brock scratched his head. "Is that all you can remember?"

Sally sighed. "That's it."

"Don't worry, Sally," Misty said. "You'll find your Seel."

"Well, standing around here isn't going to do any good," Sally said. "I'm going to search every inch of this place."

"We'll look for Seel, too!" Brock called after her as she walked away.

"We'll search for Seel while we think of an act for me," Ash reminded him. "I'm still going to enter this contest."

Misty shook her head. "Ash, you can't win everything, you know. Why don't you face it? You don't have what it takes to enter a talent show."

Just then, Gary walked by. He heard Misty's words and broke into a hu

"Listen to your friend, Ash," Gary taunted him. "Don't even bother to enter. You'll only lose to me — as usual."

As Gary walked away, Ash felt anger build inside him.

"That's it!" Ash said, thrusting his fist in the air. "I'm going to win this contest, no matter what I have to do!"

4

Team Rocket's Secret Weapon

Ash was miserable inside the rehearsal hall, but just outside, there were two happy people and one very happy Pokémon.

One was a teenage girl with long, red hair.

One was a teenage boy with purple hair and green eyes.

The Pokémon was a white, catlike Pokémon that walked on two legs.

They were Jessie, James, and Meowth.

Team Rocket!

This trio of troublemakers was on a mis-

sion: to steal rare Pokémon for their boss, Giovanni. The Pokémon they wanted most of all was Ash's Pikachu.

"I can't believe it!" James said. "The boss's new invention works!"

Jessie, James and Meowth huddled together in a circle. In the center sat a frightened Water Pokémon. A Seel. The Seel looked like it was in a daze.

"It works all right," Jessie said. "But we shouldn't talk about it here. It's too crowded. Let's get back to our hideout."

Team Rocket shoved the dazed Seel into a sack and hurried down the street.

They all turned the corner and entered a store. Musical instruments were displayed in the windows. A sign above the store read G's MUSIC STORE.

Once inside, Meowth closed the shades. James released the Seel. And Jessie held up a gold flute. It glittered in the lamplight.

"This flute works like a charm," Jessie said, her eyes gleaming. "The boss is a genius. All I have to do is play a tune, and Pokémon leave their trainers and come right to us."

"*Meowth!* It's *flute*-tastic!" Meowth said.

"Meowth's right," James said. "It's so easy to *steal* a *Seel*!"

Meowth laughed at James's rhyme. "You're a poet and you didn't know it!" the Pokémon said.

James got a dreamy look in his eyes. "Maybe I can read my poetry in the talent show," he said. "I can see it now:

The Amazing *James!*

His Fabulous Rhymes Will Make You *Insane.*"

Jessie bopped James on the head with the flute.

"James doesn't rhyme with insane, you poor excuse for a poet," she said. "Besides, I'm the one who's going to enter the talent show. I'll play this flute, and all the Pokémon will leave their trainers and follow me onto the stage."

"Right!" Meowth said. "Then they'll fall into the secret trapdoor we rigged up there. James and I will scoop them up . . ."

". . . and we'll have more Pokémon than we can handle!" James said.

"Exactly!" Jessie said. "So you two had better not mess this up."

"Don't be silly, Jess," James said. "There's no way this plan can go wrong."

"You're forgetting one thing," Meowth said. "You need a Pokémon in your talent show act. Those are the rules."

Jessie's face clouded. "That's right," she said. "I wonder which Pokémon to choose?"

Meowth cleared its throat. It danced a little tap dance. It did a back flip. Then it landed in a split.

"I've got it!" Jessie said.

"Yes?" Meowth asked hopefully.

Jessie took out a Poké Ball. She threw the ball, and a large, pink Pokémon popped out.

"Lickitung can accompany me on the piano," Jessie said. "Right, Lickitung?"

Lickitung unrolled its long, sticky tongue. It flopped its tongue onto a piano in the store. It licked the keys, plunking out a strange tune.

"Just perfect!" Jessie said, beaming.

But Meowth looked upset. So did James.

"How come we don't get to be in the talent show?" Meowth and James moaned together.

"*Seeeeel,*" came the answer in a deep voice.

Jessie, James, and Meowth spun around. The Water Pokémon was glaring at them. It didn't look dazed anymore.

"What's the *deal* with that *Seel*?" James asked. Then he smiled. "Hey, I made another rhyme."

Jessie bopped him on the head again. "Rhyme time's over, James. It looks like the Seel has woken up from the flute's spell."

"*Seeeel,*" the Pokémon replied angrily.

James took a Poké Ball from his pocket.

"No problem," he said. "I'll just *seal* that *Seel* inside this ball."

James tossed the Poké Ball at the Seel.

Seel butted the ball away with its head.

"*Meowth!* This isn't going to be so easy," Meowth said.

Seel slid across the floor toward James.

"Nice Seel," James said nervously. "Good Seel."

Seel lowered its head and picked up James. Then it began to spin James around on its nose, as if James were a giant ball.

"Do something!" James yelled as he spun around and around.

Meowth sprang into attack position. But before it could lunge, Seel tossed James into the air.

James flew across the room and crashed through the front door.

"*Seel!*" The Water Pokémon sped through the open door and down the street.

"It's getting away!" Meowth cried. It started to chase after the Water Pokémon.

Jessie stopped Meowth.

"Let it go," Jessie said. "We were just testing out the flute today, anyway. Tomorrow night, that Seel will be ours."

"You're right Jess," James said. "And so will all the other Pokémon in town!"

5

Brock Rocks!

At the end of the day, Ash and his friends found a campsite in the town park. As the sun set, they set up their sleeping bags. Misty built a campfire, and Brock cooked dinner.

Pikachu and Togepi played hide-and-seek in the sleeping bags.

Ash sat cross-legged in front of the fire, deep in thought. He *had* to come up with an act for the talent competition!

"Maybe I can sing," Ash said. He cleared his throat. *"The Poké trainer went to town, riding on a Ponyta. He stuck a Gym Badge in his cap and called it —"*

"*Pikaaaa!*" Pikachu cried. Pikachu and Togepi were holding their ears and frowning.

"Ash, stop making that terrible racket!" Misty said.

Ash sighed. "It wasn't that bad, was it?" he asked.

Pikachu and Togepi nodded their heads.

Brock set a plate of food in front of Ash. "Cheer up, Ash," Brock said. "You've won lots of contests. You've earned lots of badges. Why is this one so important?"

Ash lowered his eyes. "I want to beat Gary," Ash muttered. "He's never going to let me forget this if he wins."

Brock shook his head. "Gary only wins if you let him bother you," he pointed out. "If you ignore him, then you're the winner."

Ash didn't look convinced.

"Still," Misty said. "Gary is pretty annoying."

"You can say that again," Ash agreed.

The friends dug into their delicious supper. Pikachu and Togepi ate special Pokémon food that Brock had prepared for them.

When they were finished, Brock cleared the plates. "I'll do the dishes," he volunteered.

"Squirtle can help," Ash said. He released Squirtle from its Poké Ball. "Squirtle, help Brock with the dishes!"

"Squirtle!" said the Water Pokémon.

Squirtle filled a basin with water. Brock washed the dishes in the basin, and Squirtle rinsed them off with sprays of water.

Ash decided not to worry about the con-

test. He played hide-and-seek with Pikachu and Togepi instead.

Ash was hiding in a sleeping bag when a beautiful melody filled the air.

"Hey, Geodude, don't try so hard. Take that rock pile, and lift it higher . . ."

Ash poked his head out of the sleeping bag. It was Brock, singing a song!

Misty heard it, too.

"Wow, Brock," Misty said. "You have a great singing voice. I never noticed it before."

Brock blushed. "I always like to sing when I work," he said.

Ash jumped to his feet. "That's it!" Ash said. "Brock, *you* can enter the talent competition!"

Brock looked unsure. "I don't know, Ash," Brock said. "I've never sung in front of people before."

"You'll be great!" Ash said.

"Don't forget," Brock said. "I need Pokémon in the act, too."

Now Misty looked excited. "Brock, I think Ash is on to something. We can all help. It will be fun!"

"What do you mean?" Brock asked.

"I used to perform with my sisters at the Cerulean City Gym, remember?" Misty pointed out. "We had to swim, make the music, design the costumes, do everything ourselves. I think I can put together an act for us."

"What do you say, Brock?" Ash asked. "We can all be in this competition together."

Brock hesitated. "All right," he finally said. "I'll give it a try."

"Great!" said Misty. "Watch Togepi. I'll be right back."

Misty sped off down the street. Ash and Brock finished cleaning up the campsite.

Almost a half hour later, Misty came back to the park. A guitar was slung over her shoulder. In her arms she carried a pair of cymbals, a set of bongo drums, and a pole with silver chimes attached.

"Where'd you get this stuff?" Ash asked.

"I rented it from a music store I noticed down the street," Misty said. "The owners were kind of weird, though." She shrugged. "Anyway, I think I got what we need."

She set up the chimes so that the pole

stood on two legs in the ground. She handed the cymbals to Ash.

"Brock, call on Geodude," Misty said.

"Sure," Brock said. He opened Geodude's Poké Ball.

Geodude looked like a big, round, rock with two strong, muscular arms.

"Geodude!" it said in a deep voice.

Then Misty threw a Poké Ball. A Water Pokémon that looked like a blue-green sea-horse popped out.

"Horsea!" said the Pokémon.

"Okay," Misty said. "Here's what we'll do. I'll play guitar. Brock will sing. Geodude can bang out the beat on the drums. Pikachu and Togepi can dance. And Horsea will play the chimes."

"How does it do that?" Brock asked.

"Just watch," Misty said.

Horsea shot quick streams of water out of its snout. The streams hit the chimes one by one, making them ring. It played a short and pretty tune.

"Cool!" Ash said. He looked at his cymbals. "What do I do with these?"

Misty avoided his eyes. "Uh, you bang them when the song is over."

"That's it?" Ash asked.

"Yeah," Misty said. "But it's a very important job. You're like the grand finale."

Ash brightened. "Yeah, you're right. Just as long as I'm in the act that's going to beat Gary!"

"We won't beat Gary unless we rehearse," Misty said.

"Right!" Brock said. "So what song should we do?"

"Well, it's a Pokémon competition," Ash said. "Why don't we do the Pokémon trainers' song?"

"Great idea!" Misty said. "Geodude, hit it!"

Geodude bounced up and down, setting the beat.

Brock started to sing.

*"I want to be the very best,
like no one ever was . . ."*

Misty closed her eyes as she played the guitar.

Geodude drummed to the beat.

Horsea shot water at the chimes.

Pikachu and Togepi danced to the music.

Ash waited for the last line to play his part.

"Gotta catch 'em all, Pokémon!"

Bang! Ash crashed the cymbals.

"That was great!" Misty said. "We just might beat Gary after all."

Misty and Brock put Horsea and Geodude back inside their Poké Balls.

"Get some rest," Misty told them. "We've got a big day tomorrow!"

Ash couldn't wait until the talent show!

Suddenly, another melody filled the night air.

A strange melody.

"What's that?" Ash asked.

Misty and Brock listened.

"It sounds like a Poké Flute," Brock said. "But I've never heard anything exactly like it before."

Ash turned to Pikachu. "What do you think, Pika —"

Ash gasped.

Pikachu and Togepi were walking out of the campsite, toward the sound of the music.

Ash dove after them.

"Where are you two going?" he asked, grabbing them both in his arms.

Misty quickly snatched Togepi and put the baby Pokémon safely inside her backpack.

But Pikachu struggled to get out of Ash's arms. It ran toward the music again.

"Pikachu!" Ash cried. "Come back!"

6

Save Pikachu!

"Bulbasaur, I choose you!" Ash yelled. He threw a Poké Ball, and a Pokémon that resembled a small dinosaur appeared.

"Bulbasaur, use your Vine Whip to get Pikachu!" Ash cried.

"Bulba — saur!"

The green plant bulb on Bulbasaur's back opened up, and two long vines shot out. They reached out and wrapped around Pikachu.

"Way to go, Bulbasaur!" Ash said. "Now bring Pikachu back to me."

But Bulbasaur didn't obey. Instead, it

slowly lowered Pikachu to the ground. Then Bulbasaur and Pikachu both walked toward the sound of the music.

Ash ran after them.

"Ash, I think the flute music has them under some kind of spell," Brock said, running behind him. "We need to make the sound stop somehow."

Ash stopped. "I think I know what to do," he said. He started singing as loud as he could. *"The Poké trainer went to town, riding on his Ponyta . . ."*

Ash's off-key voice drowned out the sound of the flute.

Bulbasaur moaned. Pikachu held its ears. Then they both turned around and smiled at Ash.

Ash stopped singing. The night was quiet. The flute music had stopped, too.

"Pika!" Pikachu jumped into Ash's arms. *"Pika, pika, chu."*

"Bulbasaur," added Bulbasaur.

"I know you didn't mean to run away," Ash told his Pokémon. "That flute music had something to do with it."

Misty caught up with them.

"Ash, didn't Sally say that she heard some strange music when her Seel disappeared?" Misty asked.

"That's right!" Ash said.

Brock looked thoughtful. "A flute that can lure Pokémon away from its trainers," he said. "That could be dangerous in the wrong hands."

Ash nodded. "You're right. But nobody got our Pokémon. Right, Pikachu?"

"Pika!" Pikachu said happily.

"Let's get some rest," Misty suggested. "Maybe we can figure this out in the morning."

"Good idea," Ash said yawning.

Outside the park, Team Rocket was fuming.

"When that meddling Misty came into our store, I couldn't believe our luck," Jessie said.

"We should have had Pikachu all to ourselves by now," James complained.

Meowth held its paws over its ears.

"I can still hear that terrible singing," Meowth said. "I've heard alley cats make better music."

"That annoying amateur, Ash, will be singing a different tune tomorrow," Jessie said. "We'll get Pikachu, and all of the Pokémon in the talent show."

"Of course!" James said. "But what if Ash and his friends try to spoil our fun?"

Jessie grinned. "We'll take care of them," she said. "I have a plan."

7

Brock's Big Moment

The next morning, Ash and his friends headed for the rehearsal hall. Inside, Pokémon and their trainers sat quietly in folding chairs.

Sally waved them over. Her Seel sat next to her.

"Hey Ash," Sally said. "I found my Seel. It came back to me last night."

"That's great!" Ash said. "Now you can be in the contest."

Gary and his cheerleaders approached them. "What are you doing here?" he asked.

"This is dress rehearsal. Performers only."

"We are performing," Ash said. "And you won't believe our act."

"That's right," Misty said. "I'm going to sign us up right now."

Misty walked over to the registration table.

"I'll believe it when I see it," Gary sneered. He turned around and went back to his seat.

A man in a tuxedo spoke into a microphone onstage. "I'm glad to see everyone here," he said. "I'm Mr. Sullivan, the emcee and manager of this talent show. Now it's time for our next act to rehearse: Dan and his Dynamic Duo."

A boy Ash's age stepped onstage and sat behind a piano. Two Pokémon followed him: a Pikachu, and an orange-red Charmander. The little Fire Pokémon looked like a lizard with a flame on the end of its tail.

Both of the Pokémon wore bow ties. They gathered around a Pokémon-sized microphone.

Dan played a song on the piano. The Charmander and Pikachu sang along.

"Char char char."

"Pika pika pika."

Ash's Pikachu hopped up and down in its seat. When the song was over, Pikachu smiled and applauded.

"Pikachu!" it told Ash.

"You're right, Pikachu," Ash said. "That act will be hard to beat!"

The emcee came back onstage.

"Let's get Brock's Rockin' Band up here now," he said.

Brock turned to Misty. "Did you come up

with that name?" He looked nervous.

"Don't worry, Brock," Misty said. "We're going to be great!"

Ash, Misty, Brock, and Pikachu climbed onstage. Misty and Brock released Geodude and Horsea. Misty set up the chimes. Ash grabbed the cymbals. Pikachu and Togepi stood next to Brock, ready to dance.

"Hit it, Geodude!" Misty said.

Bam! Bam! Bam! Geodude banged out the beat.

Ash waited for Brock to start the song.

Brock opened his mouth.

Nothing came out.

"Brock, what's wrong?" Ash asked in a harsh whisper.

"I — I can't do it," Brock said.

"You call this an act?" Gary shouted out from the audience.

Ash tried not to panic. He had to think of a way to help Brock.

"I've got it!" Ash cried. He ran out into the audience, up to a girl wearing a top hat.

"Can I borrow this for a few minutes?" Ash asked.

"Sure," the girl replied.

The audience started to mutter and whisper.

Ash ignored them. He got Horsea to fill the hat with water. Then he took some dishes from his backpack and put them in the water.

"Here you go, Brock," Ash said, putting the hat in front of his friend. "Just like home."

Puzzled, Brock stared at the dishes. Then he broke into a smile.

"Thanks, Ash," Brock said. "Let's do it!"

Geodude banged out the beat again.

Brock washed the dishes. Then he started to sing, just like he always did when he was doing housework.

"I want to be the very best . . ."

The audience went wild. They clapped and cheered throughout the whole song. Pokémon danced in the aisles.

"Gotta catch 'em all! Pokémon!"

Ash slammed the cymbals together. The audience burst into applause. Ash scanned the crowd, hoping to see the look on Gary's face. But his rival was nowhere in sight.

Some of the girls in the audience called out to Brock.

"Can I have your autograph?"

"You are the best singer!"

Brock blushed and smiled.

Ash couldn't believe it. This was better than he'd hoped for!

Creak!

Ash looked up at the sound of the noise.

A heavy stage light hung on the ceiling, right above Brock.

One of the screws had come loose.

The heavy light swung dangerously above Brock's head.

"Brock, watch out!" Ash cried.

8

Ash vs. Gary

Brock couldn't hear Ash. Too many girls were trying to get his attention.

Misty saw the danger, too. She ran toward Brock.

"Togi! Togi!" Togepi called after its trainer.

Creak! The heavy light swung back and forth.

Ash pulled a Poké Ball from his belt. Maybe Pidgeot, his Flying Pokémon, could create a wind gust and blow Brock out of the way.

Ash threw Pidgeot's Poké Ball into the air.

At the same time, the light came loose. It plummeted to the stage.

"Noooooo!" Ash yelled, horrified.

Togepi moved its little arms back and forth.

Misty was right behind Brock, trying to push him out of the way.

Suddenly, Brock and Misty disappeared!

The light crashed to the stage, landing right where Brock and Misty had been standing.

Ash scanned the hall. Brock and Misty reappeared across the room, safe. They ran up to the stage. Misty quickly picked up Togepi.

"We teleported!" Misty said. "I'm sure Togepi saved us from that light."

The baby Pokémon gurgled happily.

Ash remembered that some mysterious power had transported them to safety before. It happened in the Orange Islands, when they were being charged by a fierce Rhydon. Misty was sure Togepi had rescued them then, too.

Ash wasn't so sure. But now he thought she might be right. He patted Togepi's spiky head.

"If that was you, then good job, Togepi," Ash said. "You saved Brock and Misty."

Brock studied the ceiling. "I wonder how that light fell? It must have been an accident."

"Or maybe it was done on purpose," Ash said as he saw Gary walk up to the stage.

"What happened here?" Gary asked.

"Why don't you tell me?" Ash asked accusingly. "Where were you when our act finished? Maybe you were busy making sure we would lose the talent show!"

"No way!" Gary said. "I was outside practicing with my Pokémon. I know we're going to win the competition. I don't have to waste my time trying to sabotage your lousy act."

Ash jumped off the stage and faced Gary. "It's not a lousy act!" Ash said. "Everyone loved us. Just admit it. You're afraid to lose."

"I don't lose to losers!" Gary replied.

"We're not losers!" Ash said.

Gary took a Poké Ball off his belt.

"Maybe we should finish this argument outside," Gary said.

"Sounds good to me," Ash said.

Ash followed Gary outside. Brock, Misty, and Pikachu chased after them.

"Ash, you know Pokémon trainers aren't supposed to use battles to settle personal grudges," Misty reminded him.

"This is more than that," Ash said. "Gary and I have been rivals for a long time. This is a test of skill: one trainer against another."

Ash and Gary faced each other on the sidewalk outside the rehearsal hall.

Gary was first to throw out a Poké Ball.

"Go, Arcanine!" Gary yelled.

In a flash of light, a Fire Pokémon appeared. The doglike Pokémon had a bushy tail and black stripes.

Ash knew that Gary's Arcanine was pretty powerful. But he wasn't worried. "I'll fight fire with fire," Ash said. "Charizard, I choose you!"

Ash threw a Poké Ball, and a giant Fire and Flying Pokémon burst out in a flash. The orange-red Pokémon had wings, and a hot flame burned from the end of its tail.

Gary laughed. "Are you kidding? The last time I saw you use Charizard, it helped you lose the Pokémon League Tournament."

Ash cringed. Gary was right. Charizard had never wanted to obey Ash. But things were different now. They had learned to understand each other.

"Charizard, show him what you can do!" Ash commanded his Pokémon.

Charizard yawned and scratched behind its ear.

Gary laughed harder. "Arcanine, Ember!"

Arcanine charged at Charizard. At the same time, it opened its mouth, and let loose a rain of hot, fiery sparks. Ash thought Arcanine looked like an erupting volcano.

Charizard flapped its wings and sailed up, dodging the Ember Attack just in time.

"Charizard, Flamethrower!" Ash called out.

Charizard flew above Arcanine and shot a red-hot stream of fire at the Pokémon.

Arcanine leaped out of the way, but not before the flame scorched its tail.

Arcanine spun around and growled at Charizard.

"Arcanine, don't give up!" Gary called out.

Arcanine bombarded Charizard with another shower of burning embers. This time, the attack was bigger and stronger and before.

"Char!" Charizard cried out as the sparks stung its body.

Now Charizard looked angry. It roared loudly, then swooped down. A huge stream of fire exploded from Charizard's mouth.

The flame raced through the air.

Before it could engulf Arcanine, Gary threw out its Poké Ball.

"Arcanine, return!" Gary yelled.

The Pokémon disappeared into the ball. Charizard's flame evaporated in the air.

Ash smiled. So far, he was winning.

"Think I'm a loser now, Gary?" Ash asked.

Gary didn't look shaken. "This battle isn't over yet!"

Gary threw another Poké Ball. A Pokémon that looked like a tall brown fox that stood on two legs exploded from the ball. It had long pointy ears and held a menacing spoon in each hand.

"Alakazam!" Misty cried in shock.

Ash gasped. Alakazam was a powerful Psychic Pokémon. It was hard to beat. The last time he faced an Alakazam he had defeated it with Haunter, a Ghost Pokémon which had agreed to help him out. But Haunter wasn't here now.

Ash guessed that his best shot was a quick, fierce attack.

"Charizard, blast it!" Ash shouted.

Charizard shot a huge blast of flame at Alakazam.

The Psychic Pokémon didn't move. It closed its eyes. A white glow surrounded its body.

Charizard's flame smacked against the glowing light. Then it bounced back, hitting Charizard.

"Char!" roared the Pokémon.

"Alakazam used Reflect to turn Charizard's attack back on it," Brock remarked from the sidelines.

"Charizard, return!" Ash cried.

Ash knew he'd need a special Pokémon to defeat Alakazam. But which one?

"Pikachu!" Pikachu tugged at Ash's sleeve. It was eager to go into battle.

Ash didn't hesitate. Pikachu was his most determined Pokémon. It was his only chance.

"Okay, Pikachu," Ash said. "Do your stuff!"

Electricity sparked from Pikachu's red

cheeks as it approached Alakazam. But before it could attack, Alakazam struck.

"Use your Psybeam!" Gary called to Alakazam.

Beams of blue light came out of Alakazam's eyes. The light hit Pikachu.

Pikachu got a strange look on its face. Then it began to dance around in a circle.

"Oh no!" Ash said. He had seen this before. Alakazam was controlling Pikachu with psychic energy.

"What are you going to do now, Ash?" Gary taunted.

Ash had no choice.

"Pikachu, return!" he said.

Alakazam stopped the Psybeam, and Pikachu ran to Ash's side.

"I guess you lose, huh Ash?" Gary laughed.

But Ash wasn't finished yet. He turned to Misty.

"Can I borrow Psyduck?" he asked.

Misty looked at him like he was crazy.

"Are you all right, Ash?" Misty asked. "Psyduck isn't the best Pokémon to use in an emergency."

But Brock's eyes lit up. "Give it to him, Misty. I think I know what he has in mind."

Misty released Psyduck from its Poké Ball. The orange Pokémon waddled up to Ash.

Gary laughed harder. "A Psyduck? You're more of a loser than I thought."

"Pikachu, give Psyduck a little shock for me," Ash said.

Pikachu nodded. Then it touched

Psyduck with one finger. The Water Pokémon sizzled with the electricity. Psyduck held its head with its feathered wings.

Ash smiled to himself. This is just what he wanted. When Psyduck got a headache, its Confusion Attack kicked in. A Confusion Attack could take down any Pokémon. Even Alakazam.

Alakazam studied Psyduck, waiting for it to make a move.

Misty knew how to help Ash and Psyduck. "Ash, maybe if you sing a song it would help Psyduck," she said.

"A song?" Ash said. "But I'm a lousy —"

Then Ash got it. He sang in a loud voice. *"Misty had a little Psyduck, little Psyduck, little Psyduck . . ."*

Psyduck started to sway back and forth. It held its head and moaned.

"This isn't the talent show," Gary said. "Are you going to battle, or what?"

"Just wait," Ash promised.

Ash kept singing.

Psyduck's Confusion Attack kicked in. Waves of pent-up mental energy hit Alakazam. The Psychic Pokémon reeled back and forth. Its eyes rolled around in its head.

"Alakazam, use your Confusion, too!" Gary said.

Alakazam sent Confusion energy to Psyduck. Now Psyduck started to spin around dizzily.

Ash and Gary held their breath, each waiting for the other's Pokémon to fall.

A loud voice shattered the silence.

"Stop this ridiculous battle right now!"

9

Caught!

Mr. Sullivan, the show's manager, stood between Ash and Gary.

"This competition isn't about battling," he said angrily. "It's about talent. About entertainment. You should be ashamed of yourselves."

Ash's first reaction was anger and impatience. He was so close to beating Gary! Why did this guy have to intefere?

But deep down, he knew Mr. Sullivan was right. "Misty, recall Psyduck!" he said reluctantly.

Misty held out a Poké Ball. "Psyduck, return!"

The Pokémon vanished in a flash of light.

Alakazam snapped out of its confused state. It stood firm, poised to continue its battle.

"Come on, Gary," Ash said. "Call off Alakazam. Mr. Sullivan's right. If we want to battle each other, we should do it on stage, not out here. That's what this competition is all about."

Gary hesitated. Then he held out Alakazam's Poké Ball, and the Psychic Pokémon disappeared.

"We'll finish this later," he told Ash.

"It's sooner than you think," Mr. Sullivan said. "The show starts promptly at seven. I expect to see you both there — and no more battles!"

"Yes, sir," Ash and Gary muttered.

Gary headed back to the rehearsal hall. Misty and Brock approached Ash.

"You did the right thing," Misty said. "Besides, how can you be so sure that Gary is the one who tried to hurt Brock?"

"He wants to win, no matter what it takes," Ash said.

"That's true," said Brock. "But he's never hurt anyone before. I think it might have something to do with that strange music we've been hearing."

Ash had to admit that Brock was making sense. "Maybe we should check it out," he said.

"But the contest starts in a few hours," Misty said. "We've got to feed and groom our Pokémon."

"You and Brock can take care of that," Ash said. "Pikachu and I will do a little investigating. If somebody is trying to hurt us or our Pokémon, we need to find out before the show starts."

Brock agreed. "You're right Ash. We'll meet you and Pikachu back at the campsite at six-thirty."

Misty and Brock took off toward the park.

Ash turned to Pikachu. "What do you think about all this?" he asked his Pokémon.

"Pika pika chu. Pikachu," Pikachu said.

"So you think this has something to do with that flute music, too?" Ash asked.

Pikachu nodded.

Ash thought. "Misty said there was a music store near here. Maybe we could ask them if anyone has bought any flutes lately."

"Pikachu!" agreed Pikachu.

It didn't take long for Ash and Pikachu to find the store. A bell jingled as they walked inside.

A teenage boy and girl stood behind the counter. They wore long, blue coats and thick, black glasses. They seemed startled to see Ash and Pikachu.

"Sorry, we're closed," said the girl, pushing Ash toward the door.

"We're getting ready for the Pokémon

talent show," added the boy.

Ash spun around. "That's why we're here. We think somebody is planning to do something to ruin the talent show," he said. "It has something to do with a flute. We thought you could help us."

The boy and girl looked at each other.

"I don't know if we can help you," said the girl. She casually walked to the door, locking it shut. "But you can help us!"

At the same time, the boy and girl took off their glasses and threw off their long coats. Underneath, they wore white uniforms, emblazoned with a red letter "R."

"Team Rocket!" Ash cried. He grabbed Pikachu. "So you're behind all this!" He scanned the room, looking for a way to escape.

Jessie laughed. "I'd say you were clever, if you weren't so stupid," she said. You won't be able to stop us now!"

"Why not?" Ash asked.

"*Meowth!* Because

you're going to be *tied up* tonight!" Meowth cried, popping up from behind the counter. The Pokémon held thick cords in its hands.

Before Ash could protest, Jessie, James, and Meowth quickly tied Ash and Pikachu in the cords.

"Big deal," Ash said. "Pikachu, blast us out of this!"

"Pika!" Pikachu let loose a blast of electricity.

Pikachu sizzled, but the cords didn't. They were still trapped.

Meowth laughed. "Those cords are made

of rubber. They're Pika-proof!"

Ash struggled to get free. "Help! Help!" he yelled at the top of his lungs, hoping someone outside would hear him.

"That sound is music to my ears," Jessie said. She turned on a nearby radio. "Too bad no one else will be able to hear you!"

"No!" Ash cried.

Team Rocket walked to the door.

"Sorry we can't stay," James said. "But we're off to the talent competition. We're going to *steal* the show."

Meowth grinned. *"Meowth!* And all of the Pokémon, too!"

10

The Show Must Go On

"My name is Gary and you can see, that I'm the best trainer there will ever be . . ."

Back at the auditorium, Misty and Brock watched Gary's act from backstage. Geodude, Horsea, and Togepi gathered around them.

"Where are Ash and Pikachu?" Brock whispered. "The show started fifteen minutes ago."

"Don't worry. I'm sure they'll show up," Misty replied. "This is too important to Ash. He wants to beat Gary very badly."

"That might not be so easy to do," Brock said, a little nervously. "Gary's act is pretty good."

Gary stood on a glittery platform in the center of the stage. As he sang, his cheerleaders jumped and cheered. Behind him, some of his best Pokémon were lined up, dancing in a chorus line. Rhydon, Exeggutor, Charizard, Blastoise, and Venusaur stood side by side, kicking their legs in the air.

When the song ended, Gary's Charizard roared, shooting fireworks into the air.

The crowd clapped and cheered wildly.

Brock turned to Misty. "Any sign of Ash?"

"No," Misty said. "And now I'm worried, too. Something must be wrong. We should go look for him."

Misty picked up her guitar and Horsea's

chimes. She and the others headed for the stage door.

"Where do you think you're going?" asked Mr. Sullivan anxiously. "You're on next!"

"But our friend Ash isn't here," Misty protested. "We have to find him."

"Trust me, I've seen your act, and you don't need your friend," said the emcee. He pushed Brock and Misty toward the stage.

"But —" they protested.

"You're the real talent in this act," Mr. Sullivan said. "Now get out there!"

With one final powerful shove, Mr. Sullivan pushed Brock, Misty, and their Pokémon onstage. The audience burst into applause.

Brock and Misty looked at each other and shrugged.

"I guess we have no choice," Misty said.

"But I don't have any dishes to wash," Brock said.

"You can do it, Brock," Misty said. "I know you can." She quickly set up Horsea's chimes.

"Okay Geodude," Misty said. "Hit it!"

Brock, Misty and the Pokémon plunged into the song. Togepi danced. When they were finished, they crowd went wild, just like they did for Gary.

Mr. Sullivan came out onstage.

"Let's hear it for Brock's Rockin' Band!" he shouted.

Brock and Misty led the Pokémon offstage.

"Thank goodness that's over," Brock said. "Let's go find Ash."

"Sure," Misty said, then she stopped. "Look at that next act. There's something familiar about that girl."

A tall, teenage girl with red hair waited to go onstage. She wore a glamorous, blue evening dress. In her hand, she held a gold flute. Lickitung stood by her side.

Mr. Sullivan's voice blared over the

microphone. "Our next act is Felicity and Her Fabulous Flute!"

"Flute?" Misty said, surprised. "Brock, are you thinking what I'm thinking?"

"I think so," Brock said, walking closer to the stage. "We'd better keep an eye on her."

Back in the music store, Ash struggled to untie himself and Pikachu.

"We've got to get out of here!" Ash said. "We have to save those Pokémon."

"Pika," Pikachu said sadly.

"I know," Ash said. "We'll never untie these cords. Unless —"

Ash's hands were held tightly to his sides, but he could still reach some of the Poké Balls on his belt. Stretching as much as he could. He pulled one off. The Poké Ball dropped to the floor.

Pidgeot, an orange-and-brown Flying Pokémon, flew out of the ball.

"Pidgeot, use your sharp beak to bite through these cords!" Ash shouted.

Pidgeot squawked, then flew over to Ash

and perched on his head. It bent down and started to chew on the cords.

In a few minutes, the cords fell apart. Ash and Pikachu were free!

"Good work, Pidgeot!" Ash said, calling the Pokémon back into its Poké Ball.

He turned to Pikachu. "Let's get out of here," Ash said. "We have to stop Team Rocket!"

11

Show's Over!

Ash and Pikachu dashed down the street. They ran up to the theater.

"We made it!" Ash said, panting. "Let's get in there and stop them, Pikachu — Pikachu?"

The little yellow Pokémon ignored Ash. It began walking toward the theater as though it were in a trance.

Then Ash heard it. The strange, spooky, sound of Jessie's flute.

"No!" Ash cried. He burst into the building.

Jessie stood onstage in a glittery evening

gown. She played a tune on the shiny gold flute. Behind her, Lickitung plunked the piano keys with its long slimey tongue.

All over the theater, Pokémon moved toward Jessie.

The singing Charmander and Pikachu hopped up onstage.

The Exeggutor that juggled with its feet followed behind it.

The karate-chopping Machop jumped up next to Jessie.

Ash recognized Gary's Pokémon, too. His Venusaur, Charizard, and Blastoise stomped out onto the stage.

One by one, the Pokémon followed the sound of the flute.

And one by one, they disappeared through a trapdoor in the floor of the stage!

Ash looked at the audience members, who sat frozen in their seats.

"Why don't you stop them?" Ash asked.

"We can't get up!" one man replied. "We're stuck!"

Ash heard a laugh behind him. It was James and Meowth. James held a large spray gun. Meowth stood at his side.

"Meowth!" said Meowth. "Our act is so good, the audience is *glued* to their seats!"

"It was so easy," James said. "All it took was a little squirt of super-sticky stuff before the show started!"

"Well I'm not stuck to anything," Ash said. He ran down the aisle. Pikachu had almost reached the stage. Ash had to think of something fast.

"Ash! Try singing!"

Ash looked up. It was Misty. She, Brock, and the other performers were trapped in a cage behind the stage.

"Right!" Ash said. His singing had worked before, at the campsite.

"La la la la la!" Ash shrieked in his terrible voice.

Jessie glared at him. She stepped closer to the microphone.

The flute sound swelled through the auditorium, drowning out Ash's voice.

Sally's Seel climbed up to the stage, caught in the flute spell once again.

Pikachu followed right behind it.

Ash tried to stay calm. He needed a solution. Fast.

Ash threw a Poké Ball onto the stage. A huge Pokémon that looked like a round, plump bear appeared and landed with a thud.

James laughed. "That sleepy Snorlax won't do you any good," he said. "No Pokémon can escape the powers of Jessie's Fabulous Flute!"

"That's just what I'm hoping!" Ash said.

Meowth and James exchanged confused glances.

Snorlax smiled when it heard the flute. It waddled over to Jessie.

"Come on," Ash said under his breath.

Snorlax took one slow step. Then another.

Then it stepped into the trapdoor.

But Snorlax was too big to fit through. It blocked the door!

"All right, Snorlax!" Ash cried.

Angry, Jessie stopped playing.

"Get that pudgy Pokémon off our trap!" she yelled to James and Meowth.

The two Pokémon thieves ran onstage. They pushed and shoved Snorlax, who was happily humming a little tune. Snorlax wouldn't budge.

Jessie glared at Ash. "You think you've won. But as long as I have this flute, I can get any Pokémon I want!"

"You're right," Ash said. He turned to Pikachu, who was coming out of the flute's spell. "Pikachu, use your Agility! Get that flute, fast!"

Pikachu ran up to the stage. It ran in circles around Jessie. She held the flute tightly. But Pikachu's attack was making her dizzy. She started to lose her grip.

Then Pikachu leaped up, ready to grab the gold flute from Jessie's hands.

Slurp! Lickitung's sticky pink tongue shot out and grabbed the flute before Pikachu could get it.

"Good work, Lickitung!" Jessie said, regaining her balance.

"Pikachu, use your Thunder Bolt!" Ash commanded.

"Pikachuuuuuuu!" Pikachu aimed a white-hot blast of electric energy at Lickitung.

The pink Pokémon reeled from the shock. It tottered back and forth.

"Get the flute when Lickitung faints, Pikachu," Ash called out.

"Not so fast," James said. "Victreebel, go!"

James threw a Poké Ball, releasing a yellow Pokémon that looked like a giant man-eating plant.

Victrebeel leaned over and trapped James in its mouth in one gulp.

"Not me!" James cried from inside the Pokémon. He kicked his legs wildly in the air. "Get that flute from Lickitung!"

Victreebel released James hopped over to Lickitung. Before Pikachu could grab the flute, Victreebel swallowed the instrument.

James grinned. "Now you'll never get that flute away from Team Rocket!" he said.

Ash had another idea.

"I can still battle you," Ash said, ready to throw a new Poké Ball. "Why don't you call out your Weezing? You're going to need all the help you can get."

"Why not?" said James. He threw a Poké Ball, and out popped a Poison Pokémon that looked like a black cloud with two heads.

Ash's Poké Ball flew through the air. In a flash, Charizard, a combination Fire and Flying Pokémon appeared. Charizard looked like a big lizard with strong wings and a flaming tail.

"I'll even let you go first," Ash said.

"How nice of you," James said. "Weezing, Smog!"

"Weezing," replied the Pokémon in a deep voice. Weezing started belching out

thick puffs of poison smog.

The black smog filled the stage. Everyone began to cough and choke.

Even Victreebel.

Victreebel coughed so hard, the flute popped out of its mouth.

Ash couldn't see anything through the smoke, but he heard the flute clatter to the ground. That's what he was waiting for.

"Charizard, flap your wings!" Ash said. "Get rid of this smog."

Charizard didn't usually obey Ash so quickly, but he wanted to clear the air just as much as Ash did. The Pokémon flapped its powerful wings, and soon the toxic smog was gone.

Ash quickly picked up the flute. He threw it at Charizard's feet.

"Charizard, melt that flute!" Ash said.

"Noooo!" Jessie yelled.

Charizard obeyed with a red-hot stream of fire aimed right at the flute. In seconds, the gold flute was reduced to a pile of steaming metal.

"Good work, Ash!" yelled Brock from backstage. "That was smart, using Team

Rocket's own Pokémon against them."

Meowth gulped. "Something tells me this show is over!"

"That's right!" Ash said. He threw out a Poké Ball. "Snorlax, return!"

The big Pokémon disappeared, leaving the trapdoor open once again. The trapped Pokémon climbed out of the pit. They surrounded Team Rocket, angry looks on their faces.

At the same time, Misty and the others

escaped from the metal cage backstage. The trainers stood behind their Pokémon.

"It's time for us to exit — stage right!" Jessie said. She tried to run away.

It was no use. All the trainers began to shout at once, giving orders to their Pokémon.

Sally's Seel spun Meowth around on its nose as though Meowth were a ball.

The Machop karate-chopped Victreebel.

The juggling Exeggutor threw James up and down with its big, strong feet.

Gary's Blastoise and Misty's Horsea squirted Weezing, soaking the Poison Pokémon.

Gary's Venusaur tied up Lickitung's troublesome tongue in its thick green vines.

Jessie ran from Ash's Charizard, as it tried to singe her with a fiery blast.

Soon Team Rocket sat in a tired heap in the middle of the stage.

"Now for the grand finale!" Ash yelled. He turned to his Pikachu and the Pikachu who sang with Charmander. "Give these guys a double blast!"

"Pikachu!" said the two Pokémon together. Sparks sizzled on their red cheeks.

Both Pikachu closed their eyes, focusing their energy on one giant Thunder Blast.

Boom! Huge waves of electricity slammed into Team Rocket. The blast sent them flying up at super speed. They crashed through the ceiling of the theater, and flew off into the sky.

"Looks like it's curtains for Team Rocket!"

And the Winner Is...

The audience cheered wildly. Onstage, the trainers and their Pokémon hugged one another.

Ash picked up Pikachu. "We did it, Pikachu!" he said. "You're the best."

Gary walked up to Ash. "Not bad, Ash," Gary said, grudgingly. He avoided Ash's eyes. "I guess I have to thank you for saving my Pokémon."

"You're welcome," Ash said, a little surprised. Maybe Gary wasn't so bad after all.

Misty and Brock walked across the ruined stage, which was covered with dust, wood, and plaster from the ceiling.

"I'm sorry, Ash," Misty said. "Brock and I had to do the act without you."

"Mr. Sullivan made us go on," Brock explained.

Ash shrugged. "That's okay," he said. "You guys were right. This contest isn't so important. I'm just glad I didn't lose Pikachu today." He gave Pikachu a squeeze.

"Pika!" said Pikachu happily.

Mr. Sullivan stepped out onto the stage, holding a silver trophy in one hand. He picked up the microphone, which had toppled over during the battle.

"May I have your attention please!" said the emcee. The audience settled down. "I think from the sound of your applause that we have a winner for our competition. It's Ash and his Pokémon!"

Ash was confused. "Me? What did I do?"

Mr. Sullivan grabbed Ash by the sleeve and brought him up to the front of the stage.

"It took real talent to do what you did, Ash," said Mr. Sullivan. He handed the

trophy to Ash. "You saved all of the Pokémon."

The audience applauded again.

"Yay, Ash!" yelled Misty and Brock.

Mr. Sullivan turned to Brock. "I still think you're a very talented young man. If you're interested, I could fix you up with a recording contract. You could be a star!"

Brock blushed. "No thanks," he said. "I'll stick to singing while I'm washing dishes."

Ash handed Pikachu the trophy. "This belongs to you, Pikachu," he said. "I couldn't have done it without you."

"Pikachu!" said the yellow Pokémon.

Ash turned to his friends. "This was fun. But you know what I think we should do now?"

"What?" asked Misty and Brock.

Ash smiled.

"I think we need to take our act back on the road!"

About the Author

Tracy West has been writing books for more than ten years. When she's not playing the blue version of the Pokémon game (she started with a Squirtle), she enjoys reading comic books, watching cartoons, and taking long walks in the woods (looking for wild Pokémon). She lives in a small town in New York with her family and pets.